Magic Ballerina™

Holly and the Dancing Cat

Welcome to the world of Enchantia!

I have always loved to dance. The captivating
music and wonderful stories of ballet are so
inspiring. So come with me and let's follow
Holly on her magical adventures in
Enchantia, where the stories of dance will
take you on a very special journey.

Darcey Bussell
x

p.s. Turn to the back to learn a special
dance step from me...

Special thanks to
Linda Chapman and
Katie May

First published in Great Britain by HarperCollins *Children's Books* 2009
HarperCollins *Children's Books* is a division of HarperCollins *Publishers* Ltd,
77-85 Fulham Palace Road, Hammersmith, London W6 8JB

The HarperCollins website address is
www.harpercollins.co.uk

1

Text copyright © HarperCollins *Children's Books* 2009
Illustrations by Katie May
Illustrations copyright © HarperCollins *Children's Books* 2009

MAGIC BALLERINA™ and the 'Magic Ballerina' logo are
trademarks of HarperCollins Publishers Ltd.

ISBN-13 978 0 00 732319 7

Printed and bound in England by
Clays Ltd, St Ives plc

Magic Ballerina™

Holly and the Dancing Cat

Darcey Bussell

HarperCollins *Children's Books*

To Phoebe and Zoe, as they are the inspiration behind Magic Ballerina.

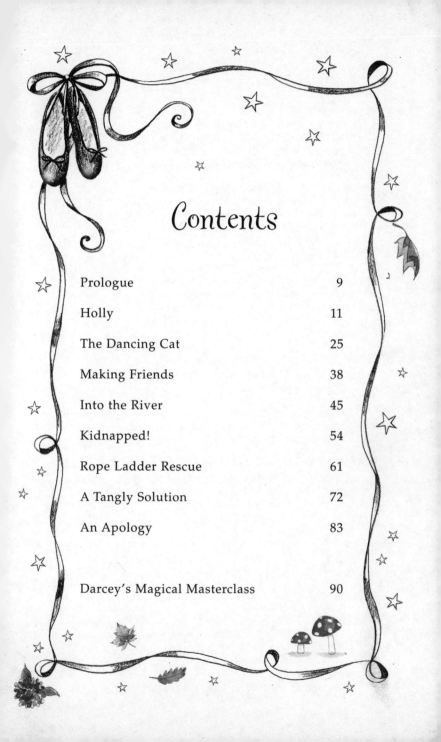

Contents

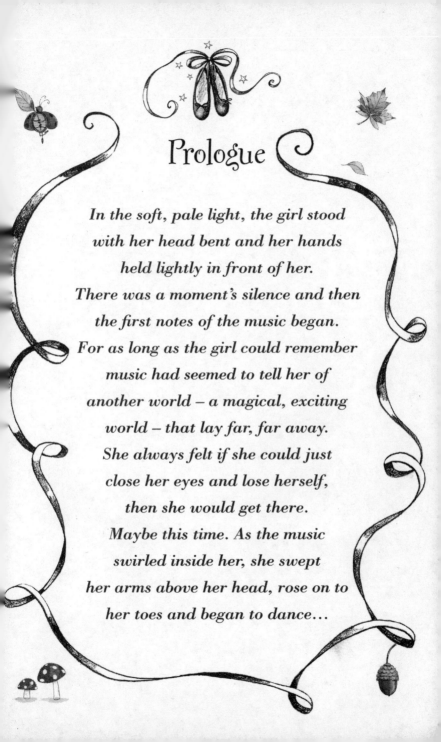

Prologue

*In the soft, pale light, the girl stood
with her head bent and her hands
held lightly in front of her.
There was a moment's silence and then
the first notes of the music began.
For as long as the girl could remember
music had seemed to tell her of
another world – a magical, exciting
world – that lay far, far away.
She always felt if she could just
close her eyes and lose herself,
then she would get there.
Maybe this time. As the music
swirled inside her, she swept
her arms above her head, rose on to
her toes and began to dance…*

Holly

Holly Wilde swept her arms in a circle and danced forward with slow steps to the haunting, beautiful music. She stopped on her right leg, one arm above her head, the other out to the side. She paused, before gracefully bringing her arm down and moving around her bedroom, turning slowly again and again, lost in her dance.

Holly loved the ballet of *Sleeping Beauty*.
Most people remembered the *Rose Adagio*,
the famous dance that the princess did before
she pricked her finger, but Holly had always
preferred the piece of music she was dancing
to now, where Sleeping Beauty appeared to
the prince in a magic vision. It had a lilting,
slightly ghostly melody. Sweeping her arms
upwards, she pirouetted around as the music
came to an end. She stopped, trembling with
the joy of dancing. Closing her eyes, she
imagined that she had just danced off stage
and that the audience were clapping wildly.

Just like they did when Mum danced it in
New York...

Sinking down on to her bed, Holly glanced
at the photoframe on the chest of drawers of

her mum, Bella. Her eyes, the same mossy-green as Holly's, were shining. Her dark hair was caught up in a diamond tiara.

Holly picked the picture up, her own straight dark hair falling forward across her face. Her heart ached. *Oh Mum,* she thought, for about the thousandth time, *why did you have to leave me here? Why couldn't I have stayed with you?*

She remembered the day she had come to live at Aunt Maria's and Uncle Ted's, back in

July. She heard her mum's words as she had left: "I'll miss you so much, darling. But you're ten now and you can't keep on travelling around with me, you need to stay in one place, go to one school and make friends. Aunt Maria and Uncle Ted will look after you and in the holidays you can come and join me or your dad just as you always have."

"But I don't want to stay here," Holly had protested.

"I know," her mum had said softly, tears in her eyes. "But you have to. We'll see each other soon."

She had kissed Holly and then she had

gone. She had phoned and emailed lots, but she was touring America and it was so far away that Holly hadn't been able to visit her. She had seen her dad for a few weeks in August when he had been performing in London. He was a dancer too, but he and her mum had got divorced six years ago, so she only ever saw him separately.

And now here she was. Midway through a new term and taking ballet classes after school. She'd started at Madame Za-Za's just before the summer holidays, but she hadn't really made much of an effort to make friends with any of the other girls. She had just felt too unhappy and, anyway, with all the moving round she'd done in her life, she'd learned it was better not to make friends. You only ended up having to say goodbye. And so she'd kept herself pretty much to herself in Madame Za-Za's class, concentrating on her ballet and coldly brushing off all the other girls' offers of friendship. To her relief, they had quickly decided to leave her alone.

Well, all apart from one...

Rosa Maitland had been really friendly. She'd left to go to the Royal Ballet School in London, but before she'd gone, she had given Holly a pair of old red ballet shoes. Holly kept them on a shelf above her desk. The words Rosa had said as she had pushed them into Holly's hands echoed through her head: "I hope you find out how special they are."

Holly frowned and, getting up, went over to them. They were old and the leather was very soft, but there didn't seem to be anything that special about them as far as she could see. Picking them up, she felt a tingle, like the faintest electric shock. Maybe she'd try them on again anyway…

"Holly! Time to go to ballet!" Aunt Maria's voice called up the stairs.

Holly put the shoes down on her desk and hurried out of the room.

Head up, shoulders down, extend the arms, remember to smile…

17

Holly and the other girls in her class at Madame Za-Za's ballet school went through the familiar sequence of exercises, first at the *barre* and then in the centre of the room.

Holly worked hard. Madame Za-Za was a very elegant woman with greying-brown hair held up in loose bun and lots of bangles. Holly knew Madame Za-Za had been a prima ballerina when she was younger. Her mum had said what an amazing teacher she

was, but although Holly worked hard, she longed to be back with her mum, learning from her instead.

"Into pairs," Madame Za-Za called as she turned to change the music on the CD player.

There was usually an even number of girls in the class so someone always had to go with Holly, but that day one of the girls was away and she was left on her own, the other girls pairing up quickly. Eventually there were just two of the newer girls left, Chloe and Alyssia. They raced past where Holly was standing in the middle to take each other's hands. As they met up, they smiled in relief.

Holly felt a pang. She didn't want to make friends, but it was hard to be left out quite so obviously. Chloe happened to glance at her and looked suddenly guilty. "Holly, you could come with us… make a three," she called impulsively.

Holly heard the horror in Alyssia's hiss. "Chloe!"

"No thanks," said Holly, folding her arms and turning away.

Just then, Madame Za-Za looked round. "Ah, Holly, you haven't got a partner. Why don't you…"

"I'll dance on my own," Holly interrupted. No one ever interrupted Madame Za-Za, who was quite strict, but Holly couldn't bear the thought of being made to join a pair and watch the other two girls exchange looks. She knew she sounded haughty, but she didn't care.

Madame Za-Za raised an eyebrow. "Very well," she said, her eyes sweeping back to the other girls. "Now everyone, I'd like you to listen to this piece of music and imagine you are two leaves on the branch of a tree in autumn, fluttering in the breeze, about to fall…"

Holly danced on her own. *I don't care. I don't care.* She kept repeating the words in her head as she let the music flow over her, taking her away and making her feel like she was falling on the breeze, turning around, using her

21

movements to express the feelings of wistfulness and sadness inside her.

I don't want to be friends with any of them anyway. I don't need them, she thought and then she lost herself in the music and thought no more.

"Very good expressive work, Holly," Madame Za-Za praised at the end.

Holly gave her a small, tight smile. Now that the dancing was over she wanted to get out of there as quickly as possible. As soon as Madame Za-Za dismissed them, Holly hurried away.

I'll put Sleeping Beauty *on again*, she told herself as she changed out of her ballet shoes. Her muscles were aching from hard work, but she knew the one thing that would make her feel better was dancing.

Cramming her stuff into her bag, she left the changing rooms.

"Holly, wait!" she heard a voice call as she half-ran down the corridor.

She turned round and saw Chloe, coming out of the changing rooms. "I'm sorry you had to dance on your own today," she said. She hesitated. "Um, you could always come round to mine sometime. I don't know many people here, either."

Holly was sure she saw pity in Chloe's blue eyes. Unhappiness swept through her. How dare Chloe pity her! She'd travelled all over the world and met more ballet dancers than Chloe could even dream of.

"Why don't you ask your mum if you can come round for tea next week?" Chloe suggested.

Holly's temper exploded. "I'm hardly likely to ask my mum when she's in America, am I? Anyway, I don't want to be friends with you or with anyone here. Just leave me alone!"

And, swinging round, Holly stormed out of the front door.

The Dancing Cat

Holly ran down the drive of the ballet school, her feet slipping slightly on the fallen leaves. It was October now and the sun was low in the sky.

Her Uncle Ted was waiting in the car outside. "How was class?"

"Fine," Holly muttered, shutting the door hard.

But as they drove home, Holly's temper faded and Chloe's hurt face refused to leave her mind. She started to feel guilty. Chloe hadn't known about her mum being away. She had only been trying to be nice.

When they reached the house she went straight up to her bedroom. It had been a horrible afternoon. All she wanted to do was dance and block everything out.

As she put her ballet bag down on her desk, the back of her hand touched the red ballet shoes. She felt the familiar spark tingle her fingers and picked them up. She would wear them. Shrugging off her hooded top, she quickly pulled them on and put on the same music as before.

Holly moved forward with slow graceful

steps and as she danced, everything else faded away. But then, moving into an *arabesque*, she became aware that her feet were tingling.

She looked down and gasped in astonishment. The red ballet shoes were glowing and sparkling!

"Oh!" she exclaimed. Bright colours surrounded her and the next second she felt herself being lifted into the air and whisked away!

Holly came to rest on a bed of fallen leaves.
The bright colours faded and she looked
around, her heart thudding. She was
standing in the middle of a wood! Red, gold
and brown leaves were lying thickly on the
ground. A squirrel scampered up a nearby
tree, pausing to give her a curious look.

Holly's mind was spinning. What had
happened?

It didn't feel anything like a dream. She
could hear birds chirruping, smell the damp
woods. She bent down and touched the
leaves on the ground. They were cool
beneath her fingers…

"Oh, my shimmering whiskers! It's you!
The girl with the red shoes!"

Holly looked up and promptly fell over in

shock as a huge white cat came dancing towards her. He was on two legs and slightly taller than her and he was wearing white ballet shoes, a black hat with a feather in and a gold waistcoat. He leaped through the air,

one leg stretched behind and one in front, in a perfect *grand jeté*. Landing beside her, he pirouetted around, before grabbing both of her hands.

"This is so brilliant!" he cried, looking

completely delighted as he pulled her to her feet. Up close, she saw his eyes were a beautiful deep emerald green and his silvery whiskers sprang out at the side of his face. "We knew the shoes had a new owner and we have all been wondering when we would get to meet you. And now I have! Oh, how lucky I am! What's your name?"

"Holly," she answered automatically.

The cat bowed. "And I am the White Cat."

He jumped into the air, spinning round in excitement. "It's amazing to meet you, Holly."

"Where... where am I?" Holly stammered.

"In Enchantia, the land where all the characters from the ballets live," the cat replied. His fluffy tail flicked over his shoulder and he pointed at her feet. "The ballet shoes you're wearing were created with some of the strongest magic in Enchantia. Whenever we are in trouble, they bring their owner – a human girl – here to help fix things. Someone from Enchantia gets to meet them first and be their friend, and this time it looks like it's me!"

Holly stared at him. Was she really in a strange magic land full of people like talking cats who came from the different ballets? Had she been sent there to help them solve their problems? Although she had to admit it sounded very exciting, an image of Chloe came into her head followed by a picture of her mum waving goodbye.

"Look, I'm sorry, I've enough problems of my own right now," she said quickly. "I just can't fix other people's problems too. Maybe another time." She turned away, wondering how she got the shoes to take her home. She tried wishing.

I wish I could go back, she thought. But nothing happened.

Remembering *The Wizard of Oz*, she clicked her heels together three times. Still nothing happened.

The White Cat walked curiously round her. "What are you doing?"

Holly turned away. She didn't want to see him; she wanted to get back to her bedroom. *Think carefully*, she told herself. She'd been dancing when the shoes had worked before, so maybe that was what she had to do?

She ran forward and turned a pirouette. *Home, home, home*, she thought as hard as she could, shutting her eyes. But when she blinked them open again she was still standing in the wood.

The White Cat leapt joyously in front of her. "Oh, is this a game, Holly? I like games!

Look how many pirouettes I can do!" He turned round on the spot so many times that Holly's mouth dropped open.

"It's not a game. I just want to go home!" she exclaimed. "I have to. For a start, my aunt and uncle are going to be really worried about me..."

"No, they won't be," interrupted the cat. "No time will pass in the human world while you are here. You'll go back and it will be as if you haven't been away."

"But I can't stay," Holly protested. "Look, will you please just tell me how I get these shoes to work and take me home?"

"You can't make the shoes do what you want." The White Cat's brilliant eyes met hers. "They'll take you back when the problem is solved, but you won't be able to make them take you back before. The magic doesn't work like that."

"Oh." Holly sat down on a fallen tree trunk. "So I'm really stuck here?" she said faintly.

"It's not that bad, is it?" the White Cat said, giving her a hopeful look.

Holly felt tears prickle her eyes. She dashed them away with the back of her hand.

"Oh, I see." The cat looked suddenly

deflated, like an old balloon. "It really is that bad." He sat down on the log and shook his head. "I don't understand it. I've never heard of a human girl not wanting to help before." He twisted his tail anxiously in his paws. "It must be me. I must have messed things up. I was just so excited to meet you."

His pointed ears flattened unhappily.

Holly began to feel bad. "It's not your fault," she said.

"But it must be," the cat muttered sadly.

"It isn't."

Holly looked at his drooping ears. She couldn't bear it. "OK. Look, I will stay and help you."

The change was instant. The cat leaped up from the tree trunk, his ears back in points.

"Oh, my shimmering whiskers and glittering tail!" He jumped high into the air, crossing his feet over and over again. "That's wonderful! Thank you! Thank you, so much!" He grabbed her hands and twirled her around as fast as he could.

Despite her reluctance, Holly unexpectedly found herself starting to smile. His excitement was infectious. "So what do you need help with?" she gasped as they stopped and the world spun dizzily around her.

The White Cat smiled at her. "Sit down and I'll explain…"

Making Friends

"It all started this morning," the White Cat began to tell Holly. "It's exactly a year to the day since Princess Aurelia and Prince Florimund got married. The King and Queen are having a party this evening and the King has said that everyone who was at the wedding has to be there tonight to do the same dance that they did at the ceremony.

"I've been put in charge of organising it. All the others arrived yesterday: the princes's brother and two sisters; Princess Aurelia's fairy godmother, Lila; the other fairies who were at Aurelia's christening; Puss in Boots, Goldilocks, Bluebeard and his wife, Little Red Riding Hood, the bluebird, the enchanted princess and all the palace courtiers as well. We started practising the dance, but then suddenly, just a few hours ago, Red Riding Hood decided to go home."

"She just left?"

Holly still wasn't sure about being in this land, but she could feel herself being drawn more and more into the story she was hearing.

The White Cat nodded. "All of a sudden. I found a note from her saying she'd decided to go home. The trouble is that means we are now one person short for the dance. I was just on my way to her house to try and persuade her to come back, but now the shoes have solved the problem. You can take Red Riding Hood's place!"

Holly felt a rush of excitement. So to help him, all she had to do was dance with the characters from her favourite ballet? That sounded OK to her!

"I can't wait to get back to the palace and introduce you to everyone," continued the White Cat. "But I think we'd better just stop by at Red Riding Hood's house on the way. I just want to check she's all right. It's not like her to let people down." He pointed through the trees. "Her house is just over there.

We could go by magic, but it won't take us long to walk and I love the woods in autumn. Oh, Holly!" He rubbed her cheek with the side of his head. "I'm really glad I was the one to meet you and that you are the new owner of the shoes!"

Holly stroked his fur. She was secretly beginning to feel quite glad she was the new owner of the shoes too!

They started walking along the path.

"So tell me about you," the White Cat said curiously.

"I live with my aunt and uncle. My mum and dad are ballet dancers." Holly quickly told the White Cat about her life.

"You must miss your mum a lot," said the White Cat with concern.

Holly nodded.

"But I bet you have lots of friends," he went on.

"Um, not really," Holly admitted awkwardly.

"Why not?"

Holly shrugged.

The White Cat spun away, jumped into the air and touched his toes, before landing lightly.

42

"Well, you've got me now!" He grabbed her hands and waltzed her down the path. Holly giggled. She didn't think she ever wanted a friend other than her mum before, but the White Cat was so much fun.

"So, tell me something more about you," he said eagerly. "What do you like? What don't you like? What are you scared of?"

Holly blinked at all the questions. "Um, well, I like ballet. I don't like school. What am I scared of? Not much really." She thought for a moment. "I don't like heights, I guess."

"I don't like water," admitted the White Cat. "I'm so scared of it. My brother, Puss in Boots, calls me a scaredy cat!" He looked around. "I know, shall we play a game on the way? What do you play in your world?"

"Um… tag?" said Holly.

"OK, I'll be it!" said the cat. "I'll count to ten."

Holly darted away through the trees to the left and scrambled up a bank.

"Wait!" the White Cat called in alarm. "I meant down the path, Holly! Not that way!"

But it was too late. As Holly reached the top of the bank, she realised that on the other side the bank fell steeply down into a swiftly-flowing river. In her surprise, she lost her balance. Her arms flailed and the next minute, she was rolling down the hill straight towards the water!

Into the River

The cold water made Holly gasp as she splashed into the river. She tried to tread water, gulping a mouthful of air as the current started to tow her along.

"Help!"

The White Cat had reached the top of the bank. Holly could see he looked terrified, but he didn't hesitate. He bounded down the bank on all fours and launched himself into the water, swimming like a tiger. Grabbing hold of the back of her leotard in his mouth, he pulled her swiftly back.

"You saved me!" cried Holly as he dragged her out on to the bank.

"Oh, my glimmering whiskers!" he gasped. "I thought you were going to drown!"

"You were so brave." Holly put her arms round him in relief and hugged him hard. "Thank you!"

The cat licked her face with his rough tongue. "You're very wet. I hope Red Riding

Hood has some clothes you can borrow.
Come on!"

It only took them a few minutes to reach Red
Riding Hood's little wooden cottage, but
when they got there they found, to their
surprise, that it was all closed up.

"I wonder why she isn't here?" said the
White Cat looking puzzled.

"Maybe she called in on some friends on
the way back," Holly suggested. She was
very cold and had started to shiver.

The White Cat noticed. "I'll find her later.
Right now, we'd better get back to the Royal
Palace and get you some dry clothes. I'll take
us there by magic." He held his long tail in

his hand and
swished it around
in a circle on the
ground. Then he
pulled Holly into
the circle. "Get
ready!" he cried.
His whiskers twitched.
Silver sparkles flew off them and suddenly
they were whizzing away!

His magic set them down in a large walled
courtyard in front of a beautiful palace with
pointed turrets and pearly white walls.

"Welcome to the Royal Palace!" declared
the White Cat.

"Oh… wow!" Holly breathed, looking round.

There was a group of dancers talking near the front door, a band of musicians, and servants setting out tables in the afternoon sun.

"Wait here a minute." The cat bounded energetically into the palace and reappeared a few seconds later with a long velvet cloak. He wrapped it around Holly. "There, that should warm you up!"

"Thanks," she said gratefully, snuggling into it. She couldn't stop staring at the dancers across the courtyard. They were all characters she knew from the ballet of *Sleeping Beauty* – the fairies, the bluebird, Puss in Boots, Bluebeard and the enchanted

princess. A few of them had noticed her
arrival and were pointing.

One of the fairies ran over. She had dark
brown hair caught up in a diamond tiara, a
lilac tutu and glittering wings.

"Hi I'm Lila, the Lilac Fairy – Princess

Aurelia's fairy godmother. Are you the new owner of the ballet shoes?" she asked.

Holly nodded. "I'm Holly."

"Oh, I'm so glad you're here." The fairy's face was worried. She turned to the White Cat. "We've got a real problem, Cat."

"I know, Lila," he said airily. "But don't worry. The shoes have solved it. Holly can dance Red Riding Hood's part."

Lila shook her head. "No. You don't understand." She lowered her voice. "Goldilocks has gone too!"

"What?"

"Sssh," Lila said hastily as several of the other dancers looked round at the cat's loud exclamation. "I've been keeping it secret. No one else knows yet, but I found a note five minutes ago saying she's gone home." She lowered her voice further. "I'm really worried. They can't both just have decided to go home. Oh, Cat. I think the Wicked Fairy might be to blame."

"The Wicked Fairy?" Holly joined in.

The White Cat looked horrified. "The Wicked Fairy is the one who tried to spoil Aurelia's sixteenth birthday, by making her prick her finger on a spinning wheel that would make her sleep for a hundred years," he explained.

Lila bit her lip. "Look, I think trouble is afoot here, but I need to ask the King something before I say any more. Wait here. I'll be back in a moment." She ran inside.

The White Cat frowned. "I wonder what she's going to ask the king. Hmm, I think I'm going to go in and find out. You stay here Holly, I'll be back very soon."

And leaving Holly in the courtyard, he hurried inside too.

Kidnapped!

The minutes ticked by. Holly watched the
dancers starting to practise the dance that
was performed at the end of the wedding in
Sleeping Beauty. It was a lively dance with
lots of skipping and galloping and turning
round in pairs. As the music played, Holly
could feel her feet itching to join in. She was
sure she could do it…

She was just edging closer when Lila came
hurrying out of the palace. "Where's the
White Cat?"

"He went after you," replied Holly, surprised.

Lila looked alarmed. "I didn't see him. Oh,
no! We have to find him!"

She ran inside the palace. Holly raced after
her. "What's the rush? He said he'd come
back."

But Lila was too busy calling for their
missing friend. "White Cat! Where are you?"

Holly spotted a piece of paper on the floor.
"What's that?" She picked it up.

*I've gone home. Tell them to cancel the dance.
From the White Cat.*

"Look!" Holly gasped. "But the White Cat wouldn't just leave!"

"Of course he wouldn't," said Lila. "Oh, Holly, this is dreadful. I think the Wicked Fairy has kidnapped him – along with Goldilocks and Red Riding Hood."

Holly's stomach felt as if it was full of icy water. "Why? Because she wants to ruin the party?"

Lila nodded. "Look, I'm going to tell you a secret," she said in a whisper. "I told King Tristan about it a while ago. He asked me not to tell anyone else, in case people got worried. However, when I asked him just now he said I could tell you and the White

Cat. He's hoping you can help. You see, the Wicked Fairy has a very good reason for wanting to stop the dance from happening."

Holly's heart was pounding. "What is it?"

"Well, you know the prince broke the Wicked Fairy's curse when he woke Aurelia by kissing her?" Lila asked.

Holly nodded.

"The truth is he only half broke it," Lila sighed. "Being Aurelia's special fairy godmother, I knew that the wedding dance had to be repeated at sunset today, exactly a year on from the wedding. If it isn't, then the Wicked Fairy's curse would fall again and everyone would go back to sleep. And this time there would be no one to save us. We wouldn't ever wake up."

Holly stared at Lila. "But that's awful!"

Lila nodded. "I'm sure the Wicked Fairy thinks that if enough people disappear, then everyone else will realise that she's up to something, panic and leave before sunset."

"So the dance won't happen and then her curse will fall," said Holly. "Oh, goodness." A thought crossed her mind. "But how can you be sure it is her?"

"When I was with the king we used my magic to look at her castle. We saw Red

Riding Hood and Goldilocks trapped in the tallest tower. It won't be long before the White Cat's taken there too." Tears filled Lila's eyes. "Oh, Holly, I don't know what to do!"

Holly's mind whirled. A picture of the White Cat filled her head. She remembered the fear on his face before he bounded into the river to save her. Now she had to be as brave and save him – and the others.

"We have to go to the Wicked Fairy's castle and rescue them, before anyone notices they have all gone," she declared. "How do we get there?"

"We can use my magic," said Lila, "but I don't know how we are going to get them out of the tower."

Holly thought for a moment. "Could we take a rope ladder?" she suggested.

"That's a brilliant idea!" exclaimed Lila. "There's a rope ladder in the store cupboard in the cellars." She ran off and came back a few minutes later with a coiled-up rope ladder. She took Holly's hands. "Are you ready?"

Holly nodded determinedly.

Lila waved her wand. "Then let's go!"

Rope Ladder Rescue

Lila's magic whisked them away in a cloud of purple sparkles and set them down behind a tree in the grounds of a forboding grey castle.

Holly peeped out. "Look, there's the White Cat!" she hissed, seeing her friend looking out of the tallest tower. "Oh, Lila let's go to the tower and then you can fly up there with one end of the ladder."

But just as she said this, the castle door flew open. A big fairy dressed in tatty black clothes stomped out. Holly and Lila quickly shrank back behind the tree.

The Wicked Fairy had cruel dark eyes and a long warty nose. Her grey hair was piled on her head and there was a long black

wand in her hand with a crystal ball at the top. Lizards dressed as footmen scampered around her. She flicked her wand. Immediately, there was a flash of green smoke and a carriage appeared. Instead of horses there were four more lizards pulling it.

The Wicked Fairy cackled as she climbed into it. "Take me to the Royal Palace!" Picking up the reins, she lashed them down on the lizards' backs. "Onwards, you fools!"

The other lizards fearfully leapt up behind her and the carriage set off down the drive.

"Come on!" Holly said as soon as it had disappeared from sight. She raced to the tower with Lila flying overhead.

"Oh, my shimmering whiskers!" The White Cat called down from the window. "It's Holly and Lila!" Two girls joined him, one in a red cloak, the other with long blonde ringlets.

"We've got a rope ladder," Holly called.

She saw a strange
look flicker across
the cat's face.

"Oh, but…" his
voice trailed off.

"What?"

The cat hesitated
and then shook his
head. "Nothing."

Lila flew up to the
window and passed
one end inside.
"Quick!" As soon as
it was secure, she
flew down with the
other end. Holly
held it steady.

The White Cat helped Red Riding Hood over the sill and out of the window. She climbed nimbly down. "Thank you!" she gasped, jumping the last few metres.

Goldilocks came next. "We're free!" she said her blue eyes shining. "Thank you!"

"Come on!" Holly urged the White Cat.

He started to climb over the windowsill and then he hesitated.

"What's the matter?" she called as he climbed back inside.

"I… I can't do it. I didn't tell you, but I'm not just scared of water. I'm scared of heights as well! You'll have to go on without me."

Holly looked at him in dismay. "But what about when the Wicked Fairy comes back?"

"Don't worry about me," he said bravely.

"You have to get back before people realise we're all missing. Go!"

Holly shook her head. "No way! I'm not leaving you." She swallowed hard and then did the only thing she could think of – she started to climb the rope.

"Holly, stop it!" he shouted anxiously. "You're scared of heights too!"

Holly ignored him. Gritting her teeth, she climbed higher and higher. Not daring to look down she stared at his shocked face. Her heart was pounding and her legs were shaking, but she had to get him down from there. "If I can do it, so you can you," she gasped as she got near to the window.

But just as she spoke, her foot slipped.
With a cry of alarm she grabbed hold of the
rung she was on with both hands. Her legs
dangled free. With one bound the White Cat
was out of the
window and
racing down the
rope ladder towards
her head and arms first.
At the same time, Lila shot
into the air.

The White Cat reached
Holly first. He held her
hands on to the
ladder as she
found the lower
rung with her feet.

"Thank you!' she said weakly, gazing into his green eyes.

Lila appeared beside her. "Come back down. I'll go behind you. If you slip again, I'll catch you."

Holly slowly backed down the rope ladder, Lila behind and the White Cat above. When they all reached the bottom she sank on to the ground, her legs too shaky to hold her up. The White Cat collapsed beside her and she stroked his soft fur.

His eyes blinked up at her. "You know for someone who says they don't have any friends, you're very good at being one, Holly."

Holly blushed.

Lila danced forward. "I'm just glad you're both safe."

"It was so scary," said Goldilocks.

"Thank you so much for rescuing us," said Red Riding Hood.

"We'd better get back," said Lila. "I just hope the others haven't realised we've all gone. You three go with the White Cat. I'll fly up and untie the ladder and follow with my own magic."

The White Cat helped Holly up as Lila flew to the top of the ladder, but just then a loud shriek tore through the air over the sound of carriage wheels.

Holly gasped. The Wicked Fairy was coming down the drive!

"No!" the fairy shrieked, her wand raised and pointing straight at them!

A Tangly Solution

Holly and the others froze in fear. The Wicked Fairy yanked the lizards to a stop and jumped out. "I saw you in my crystal ball!" she cried, her black eyes burning as she brandished her wand. "I saw you trying to escape. Well, you won't!" She pointed the wand at them again. "With this wand's strongest power, I banish you all to my highest…"

She broke off as the end of a rope ladder came flying down from the sky and conked her on the head. "OW!" she shrieked.

"Lila!" gasped Holly, looking up.

"What's happening?" hissed the Wicked Fairy, as Lila started flying in rapid circles, winding the rope ladder around the fairy. She flailed her arms and they got caught in the rope. "Help me, you fools!" she shrieked at her servants. But the lizards just stood there.

"Let's see how you like being imprisoned!" Lila flew around her legs at lightning speed.

The Wicked Fairy screeched and fell over on her back. The rope ladder was wrapped around her like a cocoon. She looked like a giant beetle struggling on the ground!

"Oh well done, Lila!" Holly cried. "That was brilliant!"

"Get me out of here!" yelled the Wicked Fairy to her servants as she rocked from side to side.

"Well, shimmering whiskers, it looks like no one is going to help you," said the White

Cat with a grin. "Maybe you should have said please!"

The Wicked Fairy shrieked in fury and drummed her feet on the ground.

Holly looked at the sky and realised that the sun was setting. The Wicked Fairy might be trapped, but the dance had to be performed or her curse would still work. "Come on everyone!" she cried. "Let's get back to the palace!"

° ☉ ˙*. ☆ ˳☉˙*. ☆ ˳☉˙*. ☆ ˳☉˙*. °

The White Cat and Lila's magic whisked them away. A crowd of dancers rushed towards them as they landed in the courtyard.

"It's Red Riding Hood!"

"And Goldilocks!"

"Where have you all been? We were just getting worried about you!"

The hubbub of voices rose.

"We'll explain later!" the White Cat exclaimed. "But the sun is about to set and we have to do the dance now!"

Holly realised there was music playing and the tables around the courtyard had now been laid out with plates of food and massive jugs of fruit punch. A trumpeter rang out a loud fanfare.

"Quick! Into your positions!" cried the cat. "There's no time to waste."

Everyone dashed to stand around the courtyard, hands held elegantly, faces turned expectantly to the palace doors. The door

was opened by a page and the King and
Queen stepped through.

The crowd all bowed.

Holly joined in with the White Cat and
Lila. She didn't have a clue what she was
doing, but it was just so amazing to be here,
watching everything.

The King looked in their direction. Lila nodded at him as if to say it's all right. Holly saw him breathe a sigh of relief and his mouth moved in a silent thank you.

With a beaming smile, he led the Queen to where two golden thrones had been set. As they sat down there was another fanfare and Princess Aurelia and Prince Florimund appeared in the doorway.

Holly caught her breath. The princess had long dark wavy hair and big blue eyes. She was very beautiful. The music changed and the princess ran into the centre of the courtyard and turned a pirouette. With a leap, the prince was by her side. He took her hand and they began a graceful *pas de deux*. In the final moments, the princess turned

with incredible speed on her pointes, moving round the courtyard and finishing with a dramatic dive towards the floor. The prince caught her and then Aurelia danced away, beckoning everyone to join in. The music changed again becoming bold and lively.

They all formed a circle and began to dance
the graceful dance that Holly had seen them
practising earlier.

The White Cat pulled her into the dance
too. Holly eagerly joined in. With one hand
holding the White Cat's and the other
extended elegantly out to the side, she ran
and skipped, ran and
skipped. He
turned her
under his arm
and then they
all jumped to
the side…

Suddenly the
sun set. There
was a bright flash

and silver sparkles rained down from the air. "What's happening?" cried Princess Aurelia in astonishment.

Lila smiled and ran forward to clasp her hands. "It's your happy ever after!" she said.

The music rose in volume. The White Cat hugged Holly. "We did it! We stopped the Wicked Fairy!" Holly laughed with delight. All around her were happy laughing people, dancing. Prince Florimund was swinging Aurelia round. Lila was dancing with Bluebeard, the King and Queen were joining in too. Holly had never known anything like it. The White Cat swung her back into the dance. "So are you glad you stayed and helped?" he cried as they skipped joyfully together.

"Oh yes!" exclaimed Holly. It seemed strange now to remember that she hadn't wanted to, and just at that moment she felt her feet tingling. She looked down. Her shoes were glowing. "I must be going back," she gasped. "I will come here again, won't I?"

The White Cat nodded. "And I'll be waiting to meet you when you do. We're friends forever now!"

Friends. The word rang through Holly's head.

The last thing she saw was everyone waving and smiling at her and then a cloud of bright colours surrounded her and she whirled away.

An Apology

Holly landed in her bedroom. "Oh my goodness," she breathed. "I'm back."

Her eyes flew to her clock. She felt like she had been in Enchantia for hours, but just as the White Cat had promised, no time had passed here at all.

She sank down on the floor. "You really are special," she murmured to the shoes as she took them carefully off. "Thank you for taking me there!" Shutting her eyes, she relived the last minutes before she had left. The amazing dance, seeing everyone so happy, watching everyone smiling at her and waving her off, and then looking into the White Cat's green sparkling eyes as she was whisked away.

I've got a friend, she thought, *hugging herself. A real friend*.

She felt a pang and realised that she was really going to miss the White Cat now that she was back in the real world.

As she got changed the doorbell rang downstairs and her aunt called up to her. "Holly! Someone's here to see you."

Holly went halfway down the stairs and

found Chloe standing in the doorway. Holly stopped dead. She'd forgotten all about her ballet class and the row.

Chloe looked uncomfortable. "Um. You dropped this from your bag, Holly." She held out one of Holly's pink ballet shoes. "Madame Za-Za asked me to call by with it because I only live a few streets away."

Holly's aunt took it. "It was kind of you to walk round with it," she said. "Would you like to come in for a while?"

Chloe shook her head abruptly. "Thanks, but I think I'll head off."

"Wait!" The word burst out of Holly. She hurried down the rest of the stairs. Still glowing from her adventure, she wanted to make amends. "Um… thanks." She felt herself blushing. "Thanks for bringing my ballet shoe round. It was really kind of you."

Chloe looked stunned. "That's all right."

"Maybe… maybe I could walk back with you to your house," Holly suggested hesitantly.

Aunt Maria smiled warmly. "That's a good idea."

Holly held her breath. She wouldn't blame Chloe for saying no, but suddenly she knew she really wanted her to say yes.

Chloe paused, but then to Holly's relief gave a tentative nod. "OK."

The two of them left the house. "I'm sorry about how I acted earlier," Holly apologised. "I was in a really bad mood. I shouldn't have said those things."

"It's OK," said Chloe awkwardly. "I just thought you might want to be friends."

"I do!" The words came out before Holly had a chance to think. "If… if you still want to of course." She gave Chloe a hopeful look.

Just then, a gust of wind blew through the branches on a nearby tree. A cloud of leaves fluttered down, catching in their hair. Their eyes met and they both giggled suddenly.

Chloe face relaxed into a grin. "Come on, my house is this way!" She twirled round happily in the leaves. Holly laughed and joined in.

The two girls spun down the street together, the golden leaves decorating their hair.

Darcey's Magical Masterclass

Pas de chat

This lively move means 'step of the cat' because it's light and quick - just like a cat.

1.
Lift your right leg to the side, pointing your toe and bending your knee. Place your pointed toe just above your left knee.

2.
Hold your right arm out in front of you and your left arm out to the side at shoulder-level. Then bend your left knee and jump lightly into the air.

3.
As you jump, swap legs so that your left knee bends as your right leg straightens.

4.
Land gently on your right leg with your left leg coming down afterwards and in front. Repeat steps.

Magic
Ballerina™
Holly and the Silver Unicorn

In Enchantia, Holly discovers a carousel of enchanted creatures, trapped on the ride by the Wicked Fairy. And there's just one more she wants to capture...

Read on for a sneak preview of Holly's next adventure...

✦ ∘ ✦ ∘ ☆ ∘ ✦ ∘ ☆ ∘ ✦ ∘ ☆ ∘ ✦ ∘

"I'm so glad to see you!" the White Cat cried. "Oh, my shimmering whiskers, Holly! This is the best surprise ever. You're bound to be able to help!"

"Why? What's going on?" asked Holly.

"It's the Wicked Fairy again," the White Cat said, his usually cheerful face looking suddenly worried.

Holly shuddered as she pictured the Wicked Fairy with her hooked warty nose, black wand and long cloak. She'd met her in her first adventure in Enchantia, when she'd tried to spoil Princess Aurelia's wedding anniversary. She was one of the few really horrible characters in Enchantia. "What's she been doing?" Holly asked.

"I'll show you!" The White Cat waved his long fluffy tail once and then used the end to draw a circle on the ground. Sparks shot up into the air and a mist formed inside the circle he'd drawn.

As the mist cleared Holly saw a carousel – a black iron merry-go-round with a spiky top. It was in the grounds of a dark creepy-looking castle and had some amazing creatures on it – a giant swan and dove, a magnificent stag, a brown bear and a sea dragon. There was one empty space left.

Holly looked at the White Cat. "That's the Wicked Fairy's Castle, isn't it?"

"Yes. And it's her carousel. She has been collecting all the most amazing creatures in the land and putting them on it."

"So they're real animals?" said Holly looking at the lifeless carousel creatures with their blank, staring eyes.

The White Cat wrung his front paws together. "Yes. They were all free to move about until she enchanted them. At the moment the magic is only temporary, so they could come back to life, but when the Wicked Fairy fills the final space, the magic will become permanent and then all those wonderful creatures will be lost forever…"

°ⓞ˙*˙☆˙ⓞ˙*˙☆˙ⓞ˙*˙☆˙ⓞ˙*˙°

Magic Ballerina™

Meet Delphie and Rosa too!

Magic Ballerina

Darcey Bussell

Buy more great Magic Ballerina books direct from HarperCollins
at 10% off recommended retail price.
FREE postage and packing in the UK.

Holly and the Dancing Cat	ISBN 978 0 00 732319 7
Holly and the Silver Unicorn	ISBN 978 0 00 732320 3
Holly and the Magic Tiara	ISBN 978 0 00 732321 0
Holly and the Rose Garden	ISBN 978 0 00 732322 7
Holly and the Ice Palace	ISBN 978 0 00 732323 4
Holly and the Land of Sweets	ISBN 978 0 00 732324 1

All priced at £3.99